From the Library of

Lauren Perth

Chelseah Perth

The Last Slice of Rainbow

THE LAST SLICE

OF RAINBOW

and other stories

by Joan Aiken

Illustrated by Alix Berenzy

HARPER & ROW, PUBLISHERS

"The Queen with Screaming Hair" was first published
in *Jubilee Jackanory,* BBC Publications, 1977; "A Leaf in the
Shape of a Key" first appeared in *All the Year Round,*
Evans Brothers, 1980 and "The Last Slice of Rainbow" was in
Storyteller Part Two, Marshall Cavendish Part Works, 1982.

Library of Congress Cataloging-in-Publication Data
Aiken, Joan, 1924–
  The last slice of rainbow and other stories.

  "A Charlotte Zolotow book."
  Summary: A collection of nine fairy tales including
"The Queen with Screaming Hair," "The Spider in the
Bath," and "Lost—One Pair of Legs."
    1. Fairy tales—England.   2. Children's stories,
English.   [1. Fairy tales]   I. Berenzy, Alix, ill.
II. Title.
PZ8.A266Las 1988   [Fic]   87-45271
ISBN 0-06-020042-1
ISBN 0-06-020043-X (lib. bdg.)

Typography by Al Cetta
1 2 3 4 5 6 7 8 9 10
First American Edition

To Eleanor-Jane,
Gabriel and Charlotte

Contents

The Last Slice of Rainbow

The Last Slice of Rainbow

Jason walked home from school every day along
the side of a steep grassy valley, where harebells
grew and sheep nibbled. As he walked, he always
whistled. Jason could whistle more tunes than
anybody else at school, and he could remember
every tune that he had ever heard. That was because he had been born in a windmill, just at the
moment when the wind changed from south to
west. He could see the wind, as it blew; and that
is a thing not many people can do. He could see
patterns in the stars, too, and hear the sea muttering charms as it crept up the beach.

One day, as Jason walked home along the grassy path, he heard the west wind wailing and sighing. "Oh, woe, woe! Oh, bother and blow! I've forgotten how it goes!"

"What have you forgotten, Wind?" asked Jason, turning to look at the wind. It was all brown and blue and wavery, with splashes of gold.

"My tune! I've forgotten my favorite tune! Oh, woe and blow!"

"The one that goes like this?" said Jason, and he whistled.

The wind was delighted. "That's it! That's the one! Clever Jason!" And it flipped about him, teasing but kindly, turning up his collar, ruffling his hair. "I'll give you a present," it sang, to the tune Jason had whistled. "What shall it be? A golden lock and a silver key?"

Jason couldn't think what use in the world *those* things would be, so he said quickly, "Oh, please, I'd like a rainbow of my very own to keep."

For, in the grassy valley, there were often beautiful rainbows to be seen, but they never lasted long enough for Jason.

"A rainbow of your own? That's a hard one," said the wind. "A very hard one. You must take a pail and walk up over the moor until you come to Peacock Force. Catch a whole pailful of spray from the waterfall. That will take you a long time. But when you have the pail full to the brim, you may find somebody in it who might be willing to give you a rainbow."

Luckily the next day was Saturday. Jason took a pail, and his lunch, and walked over the moor till he came to the waterfall that was called Peacock Force because the water, as it dashed over the cliff, made a cloud of spray in which wonderful peacock colors shone and glimmered.

All day Jason stood by the fall, getting soaked, catching the spray in his pail. At last, just at sunset, he had the whole pail filled, right to the brim.

5

And now, in the pail, he saw something that swam swiftly round and round—something that glimmered in brilliant rainbow colors.

It was a small fish.

"Who are you?" said Jason.

"I am the Genius of the Waterfall. Put me back! You have no right to keep me. Put me back and I'll reward you with a gift."

"Yes," said Jason quickly, "yes, I'll put you back, and please may I have a rainbow of my very own, to keep in my pocket."

"Humph!" said the Genius. "I'll give you a rainbow, but whether you will be able to keep it is another matter. Rainbows are not easy to keep. I'll be surprised if you can even carry it home. However, here you are."

And the Genius leapt out of Jason's pail, in a high soaring leap, back into its waterfall, and as it did so, a rainbow poured out of the spray and into Jason's pail, following the course of the fish's leap.

"Oh, how beautiful!" breathed Jason, and he took the rainbow from the pail, holding it in his two hands like a scarf, and gazed at its dazzling colors. Then he rolled it up carefully and put it in his pocket.

He started walking home.

There was a wood on his way, and in a dark place among the trees he heard somebody crying pitifully. He went to see what was the matter, and found a badger in a trap.

"Boy, dear, dear boy," groaned the badger, "let me out, let me out, or men will come with dogs and kill me."

"How can I let you out? I'd be glad to, but the trap needs a key."

"Push in the end of that rainbow I can see in your pocket—you'll be able to wedge open the trap."

Sure enough, when Jason pushed the end of the rainbow between the jaws of the trap, they sprang open, and the badger was able to clamber out. He made off at a lumbering trot, before the men and dogs could come. "Thanks, thanks," he gasped over his shoulder—then he was gone, down his hole.

Jason rolled up the rainbow and put it back in his pocket; but a large piece had been torn off by the sharp teeth of the trap, and it blew away.

On the edge of the wood was a little house where old Mrs. Widdows lived. She had a very sour nature. If children's balls bounced into her garden, she baked them in her oven until they turned to coal. Everything she ate was black— burnt toast, black tea, black pudding, black olives. She called to Jason, "Boy, will you give me a piece of that rainbow I see sticking out of your pocket? I'm very ill. The doctor says I need a rainbow pudding to make me better."

Jason didn't much want to give Mrs. Widdows a piece of his rainbow; but she did look ill and poorly, so, rather slowly, he walked into her kitchen, where she cut off a large bit of the rainbow with a bread knife. Then she made a stiff batter, with hot milk and flour and a pinch of salt, stirred in the piece of rainbow, and cooked the mixture. She let it get cold and cut it into slices and ate them with butter and sugar. Jason had a small slice too. It was delicious.

"That's the best thing I've eaten for a year," said Mrs. Widdows. "I'm tired of black bread and black coffee and black grapes. I can feel this pudding doing me good."

She did look better. Her cheeks were pink and she almost smiled. As for Jason, after he had eaten his small slice he grew three inches.

"You'd better not have any more," said Mrs. Widdows.

Jason put the last piece of rainbow back in his pocket.

There wasn't a lot left now.

As he drew near the windmill where he lived, his sister Tilly ran out to meet him. She tripped over a rock and fell, gashing her leg. Blood poured out of it, and Tilly, who was only four, began to wail. "Oh, oh, my leg, my leg, my leg! It hurts dreadfully. Oh Jason, please bandage it, *please!*"

Well, what could he do? Jason pulled the rest of the rainbow from his pocket and wrapped it around Tilly's leg. There was just enough. He tore off a tiny scrap, which he kept in his hand.

Tilly was in rapture with the rainbow around her leg. "Oh! How beautiful! And it has quite stopped the bleeding!" She danced away to show everybody her wonderful rainbow-colored leg.

Jason was left looking rather sadly at the tiny shred of rainbow between his thumb and finger. He heard a whisper in his ear, and turned to see the west wind frolicking about the hillside, all yellow and brown and rose-colored.

"Well?" said the west wind. "The Genius of the Waterfall did warn you that rainbows are hard to keep! And even without a rainbow, you are a very lucky boy. You can see the pattern of the stars, and hear my song, and you have grown three inches in one day."

"That's true," said Jason.

"Hold out your hand," said the wind.

Jason held out his hand, with the piece of rainbow in it, and the wind blew, as you blow on a fire to make it burn bright. As it blew, the piece of rainbow grew and grew, from Jason's palm, until it lifted up, arching into the topmost corner of the sky; not just a single rainbow, but a double one, with a second rainbow underneath *that*, the biggest and most brilliant that Jason had ever beheld. Many birds were so astonished at the sight that they stopped flying and fell to the ground, or collided with each other in midair.

Then the rainbow melted and was gone.

"Never mind!" said the west wind. "There will be another rainbow tomorrow; or if not tomorrow, next week."

"And I *did* have it in my pocket," said Jason.

Then he went in for his tea.

Clem's Dream

Clem woke up in his sunny bedroom and cried out, "Oh, I have lost my dream! And it was such a beautiful dream! It sang, and shouted, and glittered, and sparkled—and I've lost it! Somebody pulled it away, out of reach, just as I woke up!"

He looked around—at his bed, his toys, his chair, his open window with the trees outside.

"Somebody must have come in through the window, and they've stolen my dream!"

He asked the Slipper Fairy, "Did you see who stole my dream?"

But the Slipper Fairy had been fast asleep, curled up in his slipper with her head in the toe. She had seen nobody.

He asked the Toothbrush Fairy, "Did you see who stole my dream?"

But the Toothbrush Fairy had been standing on one leg, looking at herself in the bathroom mirror. She had seen nothing.

Clem asked the Bathmat Fairy. He asked the Soap Fairy. He asked the Curtain Fairy. He asked the Clock Fairy.

None of them had seen the person who had stolen his dream.

He asked the Water Fairy, "Did you see the person who stole my dream?"

"Look under your pillow, willow, willow, willow!" sang the Water Fairy. "Open your own mouth and look in, in, in, in! Then, then you'll know, ho, ho, ho, ho!"

Clem looked under his pillow. He found a silver coin.

He climbed on a chair and looked in the glass, opening his mouth as wide as it would go.

He saw a hole, where a tooth used to be.

"The Tooth Fairy must have come while I was asleep. She took my tooth, and paid for it with a silver coin. She must have taken my dream, too. But she had no right to do that."

At breakfast, Clem asked, "How can I get my dream back from the Tooth Fairy?"

The Milk Fairy said, "She lives far, far away, on Moon Island, which is the other side of every-where."

The Bread Fairy said, "She lives in a castle made of teeth, at the top of a high cliff."

The Apple Fairy said, "You will have to take her a present. Something round and white. Other-wise she will never give back your dream."

Clem went into the garden. He said, "How can I find my way to Moon Island, on the other side of everywhere? And what present can I take the Tooth Fairy?"

"Go up to the top of the hill, the hill, the hill, the hill," sang the Grass Fairy, "and put your arms around the stone, the stone, the stone that stands there. If your fingers can touch each other, around the other side, then the stone will grant your wish."

So Clem ran up to the top of the green, grassy hill.

There stood an old gray stone, tall as a Christmas tree. Clem tried to put his arms around it. But his arms would not quite reach; his fingers would not quite touch.

"You need to grow, to grow, to grow, to grow," sang the Grass Fairy. "Ask my sisters to help you, help you, help you, help you."

So Clem ran back to the house and called for help. The Bread Fairy, the Water Fairy, the Milk Fairy, and the Apple Fairy all came to the top of the hill and helped him. They pulled him long-ways, they pulled him sideways. By and by, when they had pulled and pulled and pulled, he was able to make his fingers meet around the other side of the old gray stone.

"Now you may have your wish," said the Stone Fairy.

"I wish for a boat," said Clem, "to take me to the Tooth Fairy's castle on Moon Island, on the other side of everywhere."

A laurel leaf fell into the brook, and grew till it was big as a boat. Clem stepped into it.

"Away you go, you go, you go, you go," sang the Water Fairy, and the boat floated away with Clem, down the brook, along the river, and into the wide, wide sea.

The sea is all made of dreams. Looking down into the deep water, Clem could see many, many dreams. They gleamed and shifted under his boat like leaves made of glass—gold, green, black, and silver. But nowhere could Clem see his own dream, nowhere in all the wide sea.

The boat traveled on, day after day, night after night.

In the distance, Clem saw many monsters. There was the Spinach Monster, all greeny-black, the Shoelace Monster, all tangly, the Stair Monster, all cornery, the Seaweed Monster, all crackly, and the Sponge Monster, all soggy.

But the Water Fairy tossed handfuls of water at them, and they did not dare come too near.

At last the boat came to Moon Island, on the other side of everywhere. Moon Island is round as a wheel. Its rocky beaches are covered with oysters, and black stones as big as apples. Up above are high white cliffs. And on top of the highest cliff of all stands the Tooth Fairy's castle, which is all made out of teeth.

"How shall I ever manage to climb up that cliff?" said Clem. "And what present can I take the Tooth Fairy so that she will give me back my dream?"

"Sing a song to the oysters on the beach," the

Water Fairy told him. "They are very fond of songs."

So Clem sang:

> "Night sky
> Drifting by,
> How can I climb the rock so high?
> Moon beam,
> Star gleam,
> Where shall I find my stolen dream?"

All the oysters on the beach sighed with pleasure, and opened their shells to listen to Clem's song.

The King of the Oysters said, "Stoop down, Clem, feel with your finger inside my shell, and you will find a pearl. Take it to the Tooth Fairy, and perhaps she will give you back your dream."

Clem stooped and gently poked his finger inside the big oyster shell. There he found a pearl as big as a plum. It just fitted in the palm of his hand. He also picked up one of the round black stones off the beach.

"Thank you!" he said to the King of the Oysters. "That was kind of you. I will take this beautiful pearl to the Tooth Fairy, and perhaps she will give me back my dream. But how shall I ever climb up this high cliff?"

"Sing your song again, again, again," sang the Water Fairy. "And perhaps somebody else will help you."

So Clem sang:

"Night, sleep,
  Ocean deep,
  How shall I climb the cliff so steep?
  Rain, mist,
  Snow, frost,
  How shall I find my dream that's lost?"

Then snowflakes came pattering down out of the sky and built Clem a staircase of white steps that led, back and forth, back and forth, criss-cross, all the way up the high cliff.

And so Clem was able to climb up, step by step, step by step, until he came to the very top, where the Tooth Fairy's castle was perched.

The door was made of driftwood, white as paper.

Clem knocked on the door with his black stone. When he shook the stone, it rattled, as if it held loose teeth inside it.

Clem knocked once. He knocked twice. He knocked three times.

"Who is banging on my door?" cried an angry voice.

"It's me, Clem! I have come to ask for my dream!"

Slowly the door opened, and the Tooth Fairy looked out.

The Tooth Fairy is the oldest fairy in the world. Before the last dragon turned to stone, she was building her castle, and she will be building it when the seeds from the last thistle fly off into

space. Her eyes are like balls of snow, and her hands are like bunches of thorns. Her feet are like roots. Her teeth are like icicles.

"Who are you?" said the Tooth Fairy. "How dare you come knocking at my door? I never give back a tooth. Never!"

"I'm Clem. And I don't want my tooth back. I want my dream back!"

The Tooth Fairy gave Clem a crafty look.

"How can you be certain that I have your dream?"

"I'm certain," said Clem.

"And if I have it, here in my castle, how can you find it?"

"I'll know it when I see it," said Clem.

"Oh, very well. You may come in and look for it. But you may stay only seven minutes."

So Clem went into the Tooth Fairy's castle— along wide halls and into huge rooms.

The fairy shut the door behind him, and pulled the bolt, which was made from a serpent's tooth.

Clem wandered all over the castle—up winding stairways, around corners, through galleries, up onto the tops of towers, out on balconies, down into cellars, under arches, across courtyards.

Everything was white, and there was not a single sound to be heard. Not a mouse, not a bird.

He began to fear that he would never find his dream.

"You have had six minutes!" called the Tooth Fairy.

Her voice rang like a bell in the hollow castle.

But then, just after that, Clem heard the tiniest tinkle, like water dripping into a pool.

"Look up," whispered the Water Fairy. "Look up, up, up, up!"

Clem looked up, into a round, empty tower. And high, high, high, high, far, far up, he saw something flutter—something that gleamed, and twinkled, and shone, and sparkled.

"It's my dream!" shouted Clem joyfully. "Oh, oh, oh, it's my beautiful, beautiful dream!"

At the sound of his voice, the dream came floating and fluttering down from the high cranny where the Tooth Fairy had hidden it; like a falling leaf it came floating and fluttering down, and then wrapped itself lovingly all around Clem.

"This is my own dream," he told the Tooth Fairy. "And here is a pearl, which I brought for you. Now I shall take my dream home."

At the sight of Clem joyfully hugging his dream, the Tooth Fairy became so sad that she began to melt. She grew smaller, like a lump of ice in the sun.

"Don't, don't, don't take your dream away, Clem! Please, please leave it with me!" she begged. "It is the only beautiful thing I have, in all this silent whiteness. It is the most beautiful thing I have ever seen. If you leave it with me I will give you a hundred years!"

"I don't want a hundred years," said Clem. "I would rather have my dream."

"I will give you a carriage, to travel faster than the sun!"

"I would rather have my dream."

"I will give you a bonfire that you can carry in your pocket."

"I would rather have my dream."

"I will give you a ray of light that can cut through stone."

"I would rather have my dream."

"I will give you a garden that grows upside down and backward."

"I would rather have my dream."

"I will give you a word that will last forever."

"I would rather have my dream."

When the Tooth Fairy saw that Clem really meant to take his dream away, she grew sadder still.

"Very well," she said at last. "Give me the pearl, then."

She sighed, such a long deep sigh that the whole castle trembled. Then she pulled back the bolt made from a serpent's tooth, and opened the door. Clem walked out of the castle.

When he turned to wave good-bye to the Tooth Fairy, she was sitting huddled up on a tooth. She looked so old and small and withered and pitiful that he began to feel sorry for her. He stood thinking.

"Listen!" he called after a minute or two. "Would you like to *borrow* my dream? Suppose you keep it until the next time you come to take one of my teeth. How about that?"

"Yes! *Yes!* YES!"

Her white eyes suddenly shone like lamps.

So Clem gently let go of his dream and it fluttered away, back into the Tooth Fairy's castle.

"Good-bye, Dream—for a little while!" he called. "I'll see you next Tooth Day."

"Wait!" called the Tooth Fairy. "Since you have been so kind, Clem, I'll give you back your pearl."

"No, no, keep it, keep it! Why would I want a pearl? Put it into the wall of your castle."

Clem ran down the stair that had built itself of snow. On the stony beach down below, his boat was waiting for him. He jumped into it, and it raced back over the sea, over the floating dreams, red, black, silver, and green like leaves.

But Clem looked behind him and saw his own dream waving and fluttering like a flag from the tower of the Tooth Fairy's castle, and the pearl shining like a round eye in the wall.

"It won't be many months before she comes with the dream," thought Clem, and he poked with his finger in the gap between his teeth, where already he could feel a new tooth beginning to grow.

When he arrived home, the Bread Fairy, the Milk Fairy, and the Apple Fairy were there to welcome him.

"I have lent my dream to the Tooth Fairy," he

told them. "But it won't be many months before she brings it back."

And he ran upstairs, washed his face, brushed his teeth, and jumped into bed.

He took with him the round black stone, which rattled gently when he shook it.

"The Tooth Fairy will look after my dream," he told the Slipper Fairy and the Clock Fairy. "She has it safe." Then he fell asleep.

When Clem was fast asleep, still holding the black stone, which rattled gently to itself, all the fairies came to look at him.

"He doesn't know," said the Water Fairy. "He doesn't know that he has brought away the most precious thing of all, all, all, all, all."

"If he ever learns how to open up that stone," said the Bread Fairy, "he will be more powerful than any of us."

"He will be able to grow apple trees on the moon," said the Apple Fairy.

"Or grass on Mars," said the Grass Fairy.

"Or make tick-tock Time turn backward," ticked the Clock Fairy.

"Well, let us hope that he uses it sensibly, sensibly, sensibly," said the Soap Fairy softly.

"Let us hope so," said the Curtain Fairy.

"Let us hope so," said the Bathmat Fairy.

But Clem slept on, smiling, holding the black stone tightly in his hand.

And, by and by, he began to dream again.

A Leaf in the Shape of a Key

Leaves were falling from the trees, because it was the second day of November. It was also the day after Tim's birthday, and he had a new bicycle to ride in the garden.

First he fed the snails, who lived by the garden pond, with some orange jelly left over from his birthday tea. The snails loved orange jelly, and ate up a whole plateful. Tim would also have given some jelly to the stone goblin who sat by the garden pond, but the goblin was not fond of jelly. In fact he never ate anything at all. He always looked gloomy and bad tempered. Perhaps this was because one of his feet was stuck beneath a huge rock.

"Would you like to ride on my bicycle?" Tim suggested.

The goblin's eyes flashed. He looked as if he would like a ride very much.

But that was no good either, because Tim couldn't lift the rock, which was very heavy indeed.

Tim went off, riding his bicycle over the grass. The stone goblin stared after him.

Leaves were fluttering down all over the lawn, and because there had been a frost the night before, the grass was all crunchy with white frost crystals.

As Tim pedaled about, he began catching the leaves when they floated near him, and putting them in the basket of his bicycle. He caught a red leaf, a yellow leaf, a brown leaf, a pale-green leaf, a dark-green leaf, and a silvery leaf. Then he caught another red leaf, two more brown leaves, and two more yellow leaves. Then he caught a great green leaf, the shape of a hand. Presently his basket was almost filled up with leaves. He pedaled back to the pond and showed all his leaves to the snails and the stone goblin.

"Look! I have caught twelve leaves!"

Now the goblin began to pay attention. "If you have caught twelve leaves, all different," he said, "that's magic."

Tim spread his leaves on the grass and the goblin counted them.

"That one is a walnut leaf. And that's an oak leaf. This is a maple leaf. And that is from a silver birch. This one is from an apple tree. And that is a copper-beech leaf. And here we have an ash leaf. And you also have a hazel-nut leaf, a pear-tree leaf, a rose leaf, a mulberry leaf and a fig leaf. You are a very lucky boy, Tim. You have caught twelve leaves, and all of them are different."

"What must I do now?" said Tim, very excited.

"You must catch one more leaf. And that will

give you what you want most in the whole world."

On his birthday the day before, Tim had been given his bicycle, and a lot of other presents, and he felt he already had most of the things he wanted.

But there *was* one other thing.

"Oh!" he said. "What I would *really* like is to be able to get into the little cave up above the garden pond."

There was a steep bank on one side of the garden pond—almost like a little cliff—where water came trickling out of a hole and ran down into the pond.

In the cliff there was a tiny cave. It was no bigger than the inside of a teapot. You could see into it, and it was very beautiful, all lined with moss like green velvet. There were tiny flowers growing in the moss, no bigger than pinheads. They were blue and white. Tim longed to be small enough to get inside this beautiful place.

The stone goblin's eyes flashed again.

"Ride off on your bicycle," he said, "and catch one more leaf. Then bring it here. You must bring me the very first leaf that you catch."

Tim rode off at top speed. Almost at once a leaf came fluttering down in front of him and fell right into his basket.

"Watch out!" shouted a blackbird, swooping past him, very low. "Don't trust that goblin! He means mischief! I can see it in his eye."

But Tim took no notice of the blackbird's warning. He pedaled quickly back to the goblin with the thirteenth leaf in his basket.

"Here it is," he said, and he took it out.

The thirteenth leaf was pale brown, and it was in the shape of a key.

"Look in the middle of my stomach," said the goblin, "and you'll find a keyhole."

Tim looked, and he found the keyhole.

"Put in the key and turn it," said the goblin.

Tim put the key into the hole and turned it. He

had a hard job, for it was very stiff, but it did turn.

As soon as Tim had turned the key, the goblin began to grow bigger. He pulled his foot out from under the heavy rock. He stood up, rather stiffly.

"That's better!" he said.

He was still growing, bigger and bigger.

"You promised that I should get into the cave," said Tim.

"So you shall," said the goblin.

He picked Tim up easily in his hand, reached over the pond, and put him into the cave.

"Why!" exclaimed Tim. "*You* weren't growing bigger. *I* was growing smaller!"

He was tremendously happy to be in the cave, and he began to clamber about, looking at the beautiful flowers. Now they seemed as big as tea-cups. But Tim found that, since *he* was so small, he sank up to his knees in the thick wet green moss, which was not very comfortable. Still, he was so pleased to be there that for some time he did not look out through the doorway, until he heard the blackbird squawking again.

When Tim did look out, he had quite a shock. For the stone goblin had climbed onto his bicycle and was pedaling away.

"Well, I did offer him a ride before," thought Tim.

But then he saw that the goblin was pedaling toward the garden gate, which opened into the road.

"Stop, stop!" shouted Tim. "I'm not allowed to go out there! It's dangerous!"

But Tim had grown so small that his voice came out only as a tiny squeak. The goblin may not have heard. He took no notice at all. He was waving his arms about, singing and shouting, and pedaling crazily from side to side.

"I'm free!" he was shouting. "At last I'm free! I can go anywhere I want! I can go all over the world!"

Then Tim found out a frightening thing. He

was so small that the little cliff under the cave entrance seemed terribly high to him, and there was no way down it. He was stuck in the cave.

"Help!" he shouted to the goblin. "I can't climb down! Please come back and lift me down!"

"*I'm* not going to help you!" the goblin shouted back. "You should have thought of that before. You'll just have to stay there! Good-bye! You'll never see me again."

And he pedaled right out of the garden gate.

Poor Tim stared down the terribly steep cliff at the pond below. The pond was like a huge lake. "Whatever shall I do?" he wondered. "Mum and Dad will never find me here. They'll never think of looking. I'm smaller than a mouse. I can't shout loud enough for them to hear me. I shall have to stay in this cave forever and ever. What shall I eat?"

He sat down miserably on the wet green moss.

But he had not been sitting there very long when, to his surprise, he saw four long horns with

eyes at their tips come poking up over the sill of the doorway. The horns belonged to two snails who had come climbing up the cliff. Snails don't mind how steep a cliff is, because they can stick themselves to the rock with their own glue.

"Don't worry now, Tim," they said kindly. "Just you hold on to us. We'll soon get you down the cliff. Hold tight on to our shells."

They turned themselves around. Tim put an arm tight around each of their shells, and they went slowly down the cliff, headfirst. It was a bit frightening for Tim, because they crawled so very slowly; he had rather too much time to look down. In the end he found it was better to look at the snails' shells, covered with beautiful pink and brown and yellow patterns, or to watch the clever way they stretched out their long necks and then pulled in their strong tails.

At last they came to the bottom of the cliff, and then, very carefully, they crawled around the stone edge of the pond, until Tim was safely back on the grass again, beside the empty plate, which seemed as big as a whole room.

"Oh, thank you!" said Tim. "I thought I would *never* get out of there! It was very kind of you."

"It was nothing," said the snails politely. "After all, you gave us all that orange jelly."

Tim was safely out of the cave. But he was still tiny, much smaller than a mouse, and he didn't know what to do about that.

And the stone goblin had gone off with his bicycle.

But just at that moment he heard a tremendous crash in the road beyond the hedge.

And at that very same moment, Tim grew back to his right size again.

Five minutes later, Tim's father came into the garden, looking both angry and puzzled. He was carrying Tim's bicycle.

"Tim! How did this get into the road?" he said. "I found it up by the crossroads. The front wheel is bent—some car must have run into it. And there are bits of broken stone all over the street. Have you been riding out there? You know you are not allowed to do that.''

"The stone goblin took it," said Tim.

"Don't talk nonsense!"

"But look! He's gone!"

Tim's father looked up at the empty place where the goblin had been, and at the heavy rock. It was much too heavy for Tim to have lifted. So was the goblin.

Tim's father scratched his head. Then he fetched his tools and straightened out the bent wheel. "No riding in the street, now!" he said.

"Of course not," said Tim.

He began riding over the grass again. He caught lots more falling leaves. But he never again caught twelve different kinds.

The stone goblin never came back.

But whenever there was orange jelly for tea, Tim remembered to give some to the snails.

The Queen
with Screaming Hair

Christina's parents were the king and queen of Laurestinia, an island seven miles long by three miles wide. It was wrapped in mist every day till eleven o'clock, and the laurel trees on it bloomed all year round; there were a great many of *them*. At the time Christina was five—when this story begins—the king and queen sailed away to visit their Empire, which they did every six years. (The Empire was another, even smaller, island, across forty miles of foggy sea.) The king and queen left Christina in the charge of Miss Pagnell, her governess, and the prime minister, and Crimplesham, the palace cat, who was the most important of the three, as you shall see.

A band played the national anthem as the royal yacht steamed away from the dock, and everybody sang:

"Our country is foggy, our country is free,
  Its people are happy as happy can be,
  Apart from an iceberg just once in a way,
  Our climate is mild as the middle of May,
  Our people are joyful, our laurels are green,
  Here's luck to our land, and its beautiful queen!"

When the yacht was out of sight, Christina went back to her nursery, feeling rather forlorn, and wanting comfort. Crimplesham the cat was there, in one of his dignified moods, looking particularly stripy, like a business-cat, sitting with his tail tucked tightly around his paws, and the pupils of his eyes narrowed to slits as he stared out of the window. He looked as if he had no attention to spare for

Christina. So she stared out of the window too, and soon it began to rain, which made everything worse.

A pair of blunt-ended golden scissors lay on the sill—Christina had been making paper dolls before it was time to say good-bye to the king and queen—and presently she picked up the scissors and began cutting snips off the ends of her long golden hair, which hung down to her waist. Then she snipped some flowers out of the flowered curtains. Then she turned and looked at Crimplesham, who was still staring into the distance.

Then Christina did a fearful thing. (You must remember she was only five at that time.) Afterward she did not know what had come over her—for mostly she was good as gold, and Miss Pagnell wrote *Excellent* on her report week after week. But at this moment she was seized with a wish to know what Crimplesham would look like *without* his long white whiskers. And the next minute—snip snap—the whiskers were lying in two white heaps, on either side of his front paws. It happened so quickly that it took both the princess and Crimplesham a few seconds to realize that the whiskers were really *off*. Then Christina let out a little squawk of horror at what she had done. For it had been so horribly simple to take the whiskers off; but how was she ever going to get them back *on* again?

As for Crimplesham—his eyes flashed like two arc lamps. And he began to grow. He grew until he was at least sixteen feet high, and he roared at Christina, "You little numbskull! You little ninny! *Look* at what you've done! Now all kinds of *terrible* misfortunes will follow. Why, in the name of all that's striped, did you have to go and do that?"

"I—I don't *know*," faltered Christina. "Something came over me. —Why are you so huge?" she added nervously. "Who are you?" she asked, hoping to get the conversation away from whiskers.

"I'm your fairy godfather," Crimplesham said angrily. "And I was supposed to look after you, but a fat lot of use I shall be without my whiskers. I shan't be able to do a thing until they've grown again, and *that* will take nine times nine thousand hours. Meanwhile, I hope your hair will teach you to have a bit more respect for other people's!"

And with that, he vanished up the chimney in a cloud of soot.

Christina was dreadfully dismayed—and more so, when the next minute, all the golden hairs on her head began buzzing and sneering together, in a cloud of tiny voices, like the shrilling of mosquitoes. "Bad girl! Nasty princess, to cut poor pussy's whiskers," they screamed. "For shame! Oh what a cruel thing to do!" and so on, and so on.

"I'm sorry, I'm sorry," poor Christina wept. "I'm *very* sorry, I've *said* I'm sorry," but that did not stop the voices at all. She pressed her hands to her ears and ran out into the rain, hoping to escape from them.

But they came too.

After that day, Christina heard the terrible little voices almost all the time. If she had not been a princess, they would have driven her mad. Sometimes she thought she *was* mad; for nobody else could hear them. She told Miss Pagnell about them, she told the prime minister, she told the palace doctor. "Nonsense, Princess!" they said. "You are just imagining things. There aren't any voices."

But Christina could hear them all the time; sometimes muttering, "Come on, you're not really trying with those sums!" or, "Go on, say something rude to the prime minister, he can't answer back!"; sometimes fairly screaming at her, "Eat up that piece of liver, pig! Stop pushing it about your plate!" or "Why don't you give your pony a taste of the stick?" Sometimes the voices gave her bad advice, sometimes they scolded her, sometimes they just teased. "Think you're pretty? Well you're not—just fat and plain!" A hundred thousand times she wished for old Crimplesham, even at his crossest and most dignified; a thousand times she wept when she remembered that it would take nine times nine thousand hours for his whiskers to grow again—over nine years that would be! It was no use cutting off her own hair—she did try *that*, and earned a fearful scolding from Miss Pagnell, who came in and found the princess snipped as bald as an egg. But in two hours all the hair grew back, screaming louder than ever, "Tee hee, thought you'd got rid of us! But you didn't, you didn't and you never will!"

Then a terrible thing happened. News came that the yacht had run into an iceberg. All of its crew, together with the king and queen, were lost. And so poor Christina had to be crowned queen, with a little silver crown made specially, since the coronation crown was far too big for her head. And while the crown was being set on her head by the archbishop of Laurestinia, Christina could hear a hundred little hair voices crying spitefully, "Now that she's queen she'd better be-have herself! Bet she doesn't! Let's wait and see!"

Christina simply hated being queen. She heard the voices louder than ever, nagging at her all day long.

About a year after she was crowned, however, she discovered a useful thing: The voices would pause in their nagging and teasing if she recited poetry, or if she sang songs or played the piano (which Miss Pagnell was teaching her). So, as you may imagine, Christina learned dozens and doz-ens of poems and songs; she practiced on her piano for hours on end. And when she was busy doing royal jobs, signing endless documents, or sitting on the throne being polite to foreign ambassadors, inside her head she might be saying a poem to herself, or following the pattern of some lovely tune. And in this way she could from time to time win herself a rest from the pestering voices.

Since music was such a help in keeping the

voices at bay, Christina liked to hear any musicians who came to the island. When she was about thirteen, a young violinist who was famous all over the world came to Laurestinia. It was said that when he played, even the birds stopped chirping to listen. His name was Johann King; Christina sent a message to him, asking if could come and play to her in private. Of course he said yes, but it was soon plain that he had never played to a queen before—he was so nervous that his hands shook, and he broke a string while he was tuning his fiddle.

"Oh, y-your m-majesty, I am so s-sorry," he stammered. "I am afraid that now I sh-shan't be able to play after all."

"Haven't you a spare string?" asked Christina.

"I make my own; no other strings are strong enough for my music," he said. "And I just used up my last spare."

Bitterly disappointed—for she had been looking forward so much to hearing him play—Christina said shyly, "I don't suppose one of my hairs would do?"

The young musician seemed doubtful, and all the hairs on Christina's head shrieked teasingly, "Hark at *her*! Thinks she's so clever!"

But Christina pulled a long gold strand out of her head—"That's *one* less, at all events," she thought—and Johann King wound it into place on his fiddle. Lo and behold, it sounded as well as the other strings, and he was able to play the most beautiful music, better than any she had ever heard. And—either because of the music or from surprise—the peevish, teasing voices were silent for eight whole hours after. Christina was able to sleep right through the night without their spiteful buzz breaking up her dreams, a thing that had not happened since her parents went away.

The next day she sent for the musician to say good-bye.

"Where are you going next?" said she.

"I am going to travel around the world, Your Majesty," he replied. "But I hope I shall see you again someday."

"I hope so too," said Christina, and she gave him her hand to kiss. Oddly enough, when he kissed her hand, he too was able to hear the voices of her hair, all shouting louder and shriller and more spitefully because of their night's silence.

"Oh, you poor little majesty!" he exclaimed in horror. "Hark at your hair! How can you bear it?"

"I bear it because I have to," said Christina, and she pulled out ten more hairs to give him for a keepsake. Then she watched out the window as his ship sailed away.

After that she went into the garden—for it was still early, before breakfast—while every hair on her head shrieked and yammered and clamored, "You'll never find anyone else who can hear us, don't think it! And *he's* gone for good!"

But Christina made up a little song, to one of

the tunes that Johann had played, and she sang it as she walked along:

"Poor Queen Christina with screaming hair,
  Her life is full of grief and pain.
  She'd cut off her hair but she doesn't dare,
  For she knows it would only grow again."

The hairs stopped their buzzing to listen to her song, and began again when she stopped. So then she sang the national anthem.

"Our country is foggy, our country is free,
  Its people are happy as happy can be—"

and she walked on through the fog and the laurel trees, singing so hard that, without noticing it, she left the garden and entered a region where she had never been.

This was called the Backward Area, and the people who lived there were called the Backward

People, not because they were stupid but because their feet were turned backward on their ankles. Also their skin was blue, and because of these things, everybody despised them. They lived in the swamp because no one else wanted to, and because they had nowhere else. They were rather bad tempered. Christina was not supposed to enter the area, but she found herself in the middle of the swamp before she realized where she had got to.

A group of Backward People came clustering around her, and they looked quite frightening, with their blue faces and reversed feet and disagreeable expressions.

"What are *you* doing here?" they all shouted rudely. "*You* aren't supposed to come here. And *we* ain't as happy as can be! Queens aren't wanted in our swamp! Beat it, before we kick you out with our backward feet! Get back to your own quarters!"

But Christina, looking around, could only feel

terribly sorry for them, living in such a damp dismal place, without any pleasures, and she cried, "Oh, I believe that if I were to pull some of my hair out, you could weave it into mats to lay over the swamp. Yes, look, it works! And you could twist hair into ropes to make swings and hammocks and skipping ropes and butterfly nets and kite strings and lots of other useful things, look, look—" While she spoke she was pulling out her long golden hair in handfuls, despite its shrieks of fury—and the Backward People, catching on quick as lightning, wove the hair into thick, strong, buoyant golden mats, which they laid over the swamp, so that what had been a damp dismal bog was transformed into a beautiful pleasure garden, with golden-roped hammocks and swings dangling from the great green laurel trees; and the Backward People were so happy that they knelt all around Christina on the golden mats, with their feet sticking up backward, and cried, "We love you, we love you, dear Queen Christina!"

She had pulled out every strand of her hair in her wish to help the Backward People, but now it all began to grow again like mustard and cress, and it hissed as it grew, "You think you're clever, don't you! But just wait till the prime minister hears where you have been, and then you'll catch it!"

The Backward People heard the spiteful angry voices of the hair, and they cried out sorrowfully, "Oh, you poor little queen, how can you bear to have hair like that?"

"I bear it because I must," said Christina, and she kissed them all good-bye and returned to the palace. There, as it happened, she did not find herself in trouble, for a wild bull had escaped and was rushing through the streets of the capital city, terrifying everybody. Christina quickly pulled out a handful of hairs, which by this time had grown to waist length again, and she plaited them into a string, and with this the bull was easily lassoed and led back to its shed.

Due to the fuss about the bull, both Miss Pagnell and the prime minister forgot to scold Christina about her venture into the Backward Area, which, from that time, began to be called the Golden Garden.

But this made no difference to Christina's hair, which continued to be as teasing and spiteful as ever, contradicting everything that was told her, shouting bad advice and rude words, interrupting her when she was trying to think, and keeping her awake at night. It was amazing that she managed to rule, but she did manage, and quite well, too.

Some months later the prime minister came to her with a pale face.

"Your Majesty, our country is in terrible danger! A huge iceberg is floating toward Laurestinia: It is 44 miles long, 25 miles wide, and 1,000 feet thick, and it is drifting at a speed of thirty knots; it will crush our poor little island like a grain of sugar. We had better all take to the boats and flee."

"We had better do no such thing," said Christina, and she began to tug out her hair by handfuls, ignoring its shouts and screams of rage.

"Make haste," she said. "Let everybody in the land come and plait my hair into a rope, and let our two strongest tugboats be ready to steam in opposite directions."

Now the iceberg had come into sight on the far horizon, and it was shaped like a double mountain, with two great sharp peaks, all of green ice.

"We must wind a rope around each peak," said Christina, tugging away at her hair in spite of its shrieks, "and the tugs must sail off, east and west, so as to pull the iceberg in half."

The prime minister shook his head, but as nobody else had a better idea, all the people of the island came to the palace and plaited away at Christina's hair, while the terrible iceberg drifted closer and closer, giving off deadly cold as a bonfire gives off heat. As it came nearer, all the laurel leaves on the island began to blacken, and the flowers to shrivel, and the fingers of the people as they plaited became numb with cold. At last twenty miles of golden rope were finished, and two brave mountaineers rowed out to the iceberg, climbed its slippery sides by hammering in iron pegs, and wound the golden rope three times around the twin green peaks. Next the two tugs, each taking the end of a rope, rapidly steamed in opposite directions. And then, with a tremendous wrenching creaking crash, the iceberg split in half, and the two halves bobbed away after the tugs, which steamed on, far, far into the southern sea.

But what was everybody's astonishment when, out of the middle of the broken iceberg, like a kernel from a nut, appeared the long-lost royal yacht, with the king and queen, and all the crew, yawning and stretching, rubbing their hands together, blinking their eyes and shaking their heads, as they woke from their frozen sleep. For the yacht, in the dark, had sailed straight into a crack in the berg, and had been stuck in there ever since.

Oh, how happy Christina was to see her parents again, to hug them on the quayside, and to realize that now she was queen no longer.

"Perhaps my hair will stop screaming," she thought. "Oh, if only it would!"

"She thinks we'll stop!" shouted the hair mockingly. "What a laugh! We shan't ever stop, we sh—"

Just at that moment the hair *did* stop screaming, and why? There was Crimplesham the cat, on the quayside, rubbing his fat striped form against the ankles of the king and queen, with his whiskers grown to full length again.

"*What* a good thing we left your fairy godfather to take care of you," said the old queen, glancing about in a satisfied way. "I can see that our kingdom has been well looked after while we have been away. Even the Backward People look better than they used to."

But the Backward People shouted, "Christina

did it! *She* did it! And now she deserves a holiday!"

"A holiday?" said the king and queen, rather surprised. "Why, where would she go?"

"I shall go around the world," said Christina, stepping on board the yacht. And the Backward People jumped on board too, to crew for her, and they all sailed off around the world, to find Johann King, the young musician, who was the only other person to have heard the terrible sound of Christina's screaming hair.

The Tree That Loved a Girl

O nce, long ago, when you could get four ounces of fruit drops for a penny, and might easily see half a dozen horses between you and the house on the other side of the street, there was a tree that loved a girl.

This happened in a village so small that there were only nine houses in it. They were grouped in a ring, and the tree, which was a huge oak, stood in the middle, and spread its branches over all of them like an umbrella.

The girl, whose name was Polly, lived in one of the houses. While she was a baby, her mother

used to leave her out in her cradle under the oak tree, and there she would lie, kicking her feet and waving her fists and looking up at the sunshine coming through hundreds of green leaves above her. And the oak tree looked down and thought that Polly was the prettiest baby in the world. She had blue eyes, brown hair, and pink cheeks.

When Polly grew a little older, she used to bring her skipping rope, or roller skates, and skip or skate under the tree. And she played dolls' tea parties with the acorn cups, or hide-and-seek with her friends, around the oak tree's enormous trunk. Even if it was a pouring-wet day, the oak tree took care that no drop of rain should fall on Polly.

And then, when Polly was a little older, she used to bring her books after school and sit doing her homework under the tree, while it shaded her with its branches from the hot sun.

And later, when the girls of the village washed their clothes in the fountain, Polly would be there too, and the oak tree looked at her and loved her best. When she had washed all her hair ribbons—red, blue, green, yellow, and pink—she would hang them on a branch to dry. And the oak tree took care that they should not be blown away, or stolen by nest-building birds.

In autumn, the branches over Polly's house were always the last to lose their leaves, and in spring they were the first to bud.

But girls grow faster than trees. After what seemed only a few months to the oak tree, Polly grew up, and she went away to the city to seek her fortune.

At first the oak tree could not believe that she had left. But there were no ribbons hanging on the branches to dry at night, no books laid out on the grass among its roots, no Polly playing hide-and-seek with her friends around the huge, wrinkled trunk when homework was finished. She was truly gone.

The tree began to mourn. Although it was no later than midsummer, leaves began falling from its branches. Birds who had built their nests among the twigs became anxious.

"How can we protect our fledglings from hawks and owls once the leaves have fallen?" they asked.

A wood dove flew to the top of the tree, and asked it, "Dear Tree, what is the matter? Why do you drop your leaves in the middle of the summer? Is some worm gnawing at your roots? Can we do anything to help you?"

"I am sad because Polly has gone away. I haven't the heart to send out sap to keep my leaves green, now that she is no longer here to see them. No, there is nothing you can do for me."

And the oak tree sighed deeply, as if a great gust of wind had blown through its branches. A thousand leaves fluttered off and scattered like flakes of snow. All the branches moved, and stretched yearningly in the direction of the city where Polly had gone.

"Why don't you send her a message asking her to come back?" asked the practical wood dove.

"I will send her a thousand messages," said the oak tree.

All the leaves that had fallen drifted on the breeze to the city where Polly now lived. Wherever she walked, oak leaves drifted down and touched her softly, as if begging her to return home. But Polly did not understand the oak tree's message.

"It is very queer," she said, "that all these oak leaves keep falling on me when there is no tree anywhere near."

"You must try something else," said the wood dove to the tree, when Polly did not come.

So the tree sent a dream to the village carpenter—whose house stood nearest to its trunk—asking him to cut off a branch, and make it into a gift for Polly. Losing a branch was dreadful to the tree. As the saw bit deeper, the oak tree trembled and groaned. But at last the branch was off, and the carpenter turned it into a beautiful rocking chair.

"Go to the city and find Polly," the oak tree

had begged him in his dream, "give her the chair with my love, and beseech her to come home." So the carpenter put the chair on a mule and rode to the city. But when he arrived there, he thought, "I could sell this handsome chair for enough to buy a new mule. Why should I run errands for the tree? Why should I trouble to search for the girl?"

So that is what he did. The wood dove had flown after him, saw what happened, and told the oak tree. The tree was so angry that another of its branches cracked down, split with rage, and fell on the carpenter's roof. When he returned home with his new mule, he found his house in ruins.

And the oak tree's leaves continued to fall.

"What shall we do now?" said the birds.

They asked the advice of the mistletoe, which hung in the oak tree's topmost fork. The mistletoe was growing anxious, for if the tree died, it, too, would be homeless.

"Pick enough of my berries to make a neck-lace," it said. "And carry that to Polly."

So the birds picked a hundred beautiful pearly mistletoe berries, and strung a necklace on a stem of grass, and the wood dove carried it to the city, looked for Polly, who was walking in the street, then skillfully dropped the necklace over her head.

"My goodness! Who has sent me this beautiful present?" said Polly.

But she never guessed that it was the oak tree who had sent it.

Meantime the tree waited, growing sadder and sadder.

"At least keep your leaves on till our fledglings have flown," begged the birds.

So the tree agreed to do this. But all the leaves turned brown, as if winter had come; only the mistletoe remained green in the topmost fork.

Now a young man saw Polly walking along the city street, wearing her beautiful pearl-colored necklace, and he, like the oak tree, thought she was the prettiest girl in the world. So he asked her to marry him and she said yes. They had their wedding in the city, and the wood dove watched from the church steeple and was dreadfully troubled, for now it seemed unlikely that Polly would ever return home.

But the wood dove was wrong.

For when Polly's new husband said to her, "How many children shall we have? And where shall we live?" Polly remembered the oak tree beneath which she had lain in her cradle, which had kept her dry from the rain while she played with her friends, and sheltered her from the sun while she did her homework; suddenly she became homesick for the place she had been born.

"Let us go back to my village," she said to her husband.

So they bought a mule, and on the first day of autumn, when the leaves, red, golden, and brown, were beginning to blow from the trees, they came riding back. The carpenter had left his ruined home and gone away, so Polly and her husband repaired the house and moved into it.

At first the oak tree could hardly believe its good fortune.

But when it understood that Polly had truly come back to live in the village, the sap started running through its veins, and dripped down like tears of joy. New pink buds and new green leaves began to sprout from its twigs, just when the other trees were losing their leaves, and all winter long, the oak tree remained green from happiness.

The next summer Polly had a baby of her own. She put it out under the oak tree in its cradle, and the oak tree looked down at the baby's brown hair, blue eyes, and pink cheeks, and thought, "That is the prettiest baby in the world."

Lost—One Pair of Legs

Once there was a vain, proud, careless, thoughtless boy called Cal Finhorn, who was very good at tennis. He won this game, he won that game, and then he won a tournament, and had a silver cup with his name on it.

Winning this cup made him even prouder— too proud to speak to any of the other players at the tournament. As soon as he could, he took his silver cup and hurried away to the entrance of the sports ground, where the buses stop.

"Just wait till I show them this cup at home,"

he was thinking. "I'll make Jenny polish it every day."

Jenny was Cal's younger sister. He made her do lots of things for him—wash his cereal bowl, make his bed, clean his shoes, feed his rabbits.

He had not allowed her to come to the tournament, in case he lost.

On the way across the grass toward the bus stop, Cal saw a great velvety fluttering butterfly with purple and white and black circles on its wings.

Cal was a boy who acted before he thought. Maybe sometimes he didn't think at all. He hit the butterfly a smack with his tennis racket, and it fell to the ground, stunned. Cal felt sorry then, perhaps, for what he had done to it, but it was too late, for he heard a tremendous clap of thunder, and then he saw the Lady Esclairmonde, the queen of winged things, hovering right in his path.

She looked very frightening indeed—she was all wrapped in a cloak of gray and white feathers; she had the face of a hawk, hands like claws, a crest of flame; and her hair and ribbons and the train of her dress flew out sideways, as if a force-twelve gale surrounded her. Cal could hear a fluttering sound, such as a flag or sail makes in a high wind. His own heart was fluttering inside him; he could hear that, too, like a lark inside a biscuit tin.

"Why did you hit my butterfly, Cal?" asked the Lady Esclairmonde.

Cal tried to brazen it out. He grinned at the lady. But he glanced nervously around him, wondering if people noticed that she was speaking to him. Perhaps, he thought hopefully, they might think she was congratulating him on his silver cup.

Nobody else seemed to have noticed the lady.

"Ah, shucks, it was only a silly butterfly," said Cal. "Anyway, I don't suppose I hurt it."

"Oh," said the lady. "What makes you think that?"

"It hasn't written me a letter of complaint," said Cal, grinning.

As he spoke these words, he noticed a very odd feeling under his right hip. And when he looked down, he saw his right leg remove itself from him and go hopping off across the grass, heel and toe, heel and toe, as if it were dancing a hornpipe. The leg seemed delighted to be off and away on its own. It went dancing over to the bus stop. Just then a number 19 bus swept into the stop, and the leg hopped up on board and was borne away.

"*Hey!*" bawled Cal in horror. "Come back! Come back! You're my leg! You've no right to go off and leave me in the lurch. And that isn't the right bus!"

Lurch was the right word. With only one leg, Cal was swaying about like a hollyhock in a gale. He was obliged to prop himself up with his tennis racket. He turned angrily to the lady and said, "Did *you* do that? You've no right to take away my leg! It isn't fair!"

"Nothing is fair," said the lady sternly. "What you did to my butterfly was not fair either. You may think yourself lucky I didn't take the other leg as well."

"I think you are a mean old witch!" said Cal.

Instantly he felt a jerk as his left leg undid itself from the hip. Cal bumped down onto the grass, hard, while his left leg went capering away across the grass, free as you please, up on the point of its toe, pirouetting like a ballerina. When it reached the bus stop, a number 16 had just pulled up; the left leg hopped nimbly on board and was carried away.

"You're on the wrong bus! Come back!" shouted Cal, but the leg made no answer to that.

Todd Crossfinch, who was in Cal's class at school, came by just then.

"Coo! Cal," he said, "you lost your legs, then?"

"You can blooming well see I have!" said Cal angrily.

"Want me to wheel you to the bus stop in my bike basket?" said Tod.

"No! I want my legs back," said Cal.

"You won't get them back," the Lady Esclair-monde told him, "until a pair of butterflies brings them."

Then she vanished in a flash of lightning and smell of burnt feathers.

"Who was that?" said Tod. "Was that the new French teacher? You sure you don't want me to wheel you as far as the bus stop, Cal?"

"Oh, all right," said Cal, very annoyed; so Tod packed him in his bike basket and wheeled him to the stop, and then waited and helped him onto a number 2 bus. It was all very upsetting and embarrassing. People on the bus said, "Ooh, look! There's a boy whose legs have gone off and left him. He *must* have treated them badly. Wonder what he did?"

When Cal got to his own stop, the conductor had to lift him off the bus, and then he had to walk into the garden on his hands. Luckily he was quite good at that. There he found his sister Jenny feeding her butterflies. She had about forty tame ones who used to come every day when she sprinkled sugar on a tray: small blue ones, large white ones, yellow ones, red-and-black ones, and big beautiful Tortoiseshells, Peacocks, Red Admirals, and Purple Emperors. They were flittering and fluttering all around Jenny, with a sound like falling leaves.

"Ooh, Cal," said Jenny, "what*ever* have you done with your legs?"

"They ran off and left me," said Cal, very annoyed that he had to keep telling people that his legs didn't want to stay with him.

As Cal spoke, all the butterflies rose up in a cloud of wings and flew away.

"Oh, poor Cal!" said Jenny. "Never mind, I'll wheel you about in my doll's stroller."

"I'd rather wheel myself about on your skate-board," said Cal.

Jenny was rather disappointed, but she kindly let him have the skateboard.

"Er, Jenny," said Cal, "you don't suppose your butterflies would bring back my legs, do you?"

"Oh, no, Cal," said Jenny. "Why should they? You haven't done anything for them. In fact they don't like you much, because you always chase them and try to catch them in your handkerchief."

Cal's father said that Cal had better try advertising to get his legs back.

So he put a card in the post office window, and also a notice in the local paper:

LOST

One pair of legs. Reward offered.

Lots and lots of people turned up hoping for the reward, but the legs they brought were never the right ones. There were old, rheumatic legs in wrinkled boots, or skinny girls' legs in knitted leg warmers, or babies' legs or football legs or ballet dancers' legs in pink cotton slippers.

"I never knew before that so many legs ran away from their owners," said Jenny.

This fact ought to have cheered Cal up a bit, but it didn't.

Jenny would have liked to adopt a pair of the ballet legs, but her mother said no, a canary and some rabbits were all the pets they had room for. "Besides, those legs must belong to someone else who wants them back."

Then a friend told Cal's father that one of Cal's legs was performing every night in the local pub, the Ring o' Roses. "Dances around on the bar, very active, it does. Brings in a whole lot o' customers."

Mr. Finhorn went along one night to see, and sure enough he recognized Cal's leg, with the scar on the knee where he had fallen down the front steps carrying a bottle of milk. But when the leg saw Mr. Finhorn, it danced away along the bar and skipped out of the window, and went hopping off down the road in the dark.

The other leg was heard of up in London; it had got a job at the Hippodrome Theater, dancing on the stage with a parasol tucked into its garter.

"I don't believe they'll *ever* come back to me now," said Cal hopelessly.

Cal was becoming very sad and quiet, not a bit like what he had been before. He was a good deal nicer to Jenny and even helped his mother with the dishwashing, balancing on a kitchen stool.

"It's not very likely," his mother agreed. "Not now that they're used to earning their own living."

"Maybe if you fed my butterflies every day, they'd bring your legs back," suggested Jenny.

So Cal rolled out on his skateboard every day and fed the butterflies with handfuls of sugar. They grew quite accustomed to him, and would perch on his arms and head and hands.

But summer was nearly over; autumn was coming; there were fewer butterflies every day. And still Cal's legs did not come back.

School began again. Every day Cal went to school on the skateboard, rolling himself along with his hands. He couldn't play football, because of having no legs, but he could still swim, so he did that three times a week, in the school pool.

One day while he was swimming he saw two butterflies floating in the center of the pool. They were flapping and struggling a little, but very feebly; it looked as if they were going to drown.

Cal dog-paddled toward them, as fast as he could. "Poor things," he thought, "they must feel horrible with their wings all wet and floppy."

They were two of a kind he had never seen before—very large, silvery in color, with lavender streaks and long trailing points to their wings.

Cal wondered how he could save them.

"For if I take them in my hands," he thought, "I might squash them. And they would have to go underwater when I swim. Oh, if only I had my legs! Then I could swim with my legs and hold the butterflies above water."

But he hadn't got his legs, so he could only swim with his arms.

"I'll have to take the butterflies in my mouth," Cal thought then.

He didn't much care for the idea. In fact it made him shivery down his back—to think of having two live, fluttery butterflies inside his mouth. Still, that seemed the only way to save them. He opened his mouth very wide indeed—luckily it was a big one anyway—and gently scooped the two butterflies in with his tongue, as they themselves scoop in sugar. He was careful to take in as little water as possible.

Then, with open mouth and head well above water, he swam like mad for the side of the pool.

But, on the way, the butterflies began to fidget and flutter inside his mouth.

"Oh, I can't bear it," thought Cal.

Now the butterflies were beating and battering inside his mouth—he felt as if his head were hollow, and the whole of it were filled with great flapping wings and kicking legs and waving whiskers. They tickled and rustled and scraped and scrabbled and nearly drove him frantic. Still he went on swimming as fast as he was able.

Then it got so bad that he felt as if his whole head were going to be lifted off. But it was not only his head—suddenly Cal, head, arms, and all, found himself lifted right out of the swimming pool and carried through the air by the two butterflies whirring like helicopters inside his mouth.

They carried him away from the school and back to his own garden, full of lavender and nasturtiums and Michaelmas daisies, where Jenny was scattering sugar on a tray.

And there, sitting in a deckchair waiting for him, were his own two legs!

Cal opened his mouth so wide in amazement

that the two silvery butterflies shot out, and dropped down onto the tray to refresh themselves with a little sugar. Which they must have needed, after carrying Cal all wet and dripping.

And Cal's legs stood up, stretched themselves a bit, in a carefree way, heel and toe, the way cats do, then came hopping over to hook themselves onto Cal's hips, as calm and friendly as if they had never been away.

Was Cal a different boy after that? He was indeed. For one thing, those legs had learned such a lot, while they were off on their own, that he could have made an easy living in any circus, or football team, or dance company—and did, for a while, when he grew up.

Also, he never grew tired of listening to his legs, who used to argue in bed, every night, recalling the days when they had been off in the world by themselves.

". . . That time when I jumped into the tiger's cage—"

"Shucks! That wasn't so extra brave. Not like when I tripped up the bank robbers—"

"That was nothing."

"You weren't there. You don't know how it happened!"

So they used to argue.

For the rest of his life Cal was very polite to his legs, in case they ever took a fancy to go off again.

The Voice in the Shell

Once there was a boy called Michael who was walking along the beach, thinking about his future.

"I want to be a painter," he thought. "I really want to be a painter."

He looked at the green sea, and the gray sand, and the waves rolling in, each with a white frothing crest, the white stones on the beach, the black breakwaters, and the golden hills behind.

"I would like to paint all that," he thought.

The problem was that Michael's father told him he had better not become a painter unless he could be quite sure that he would be the best painter in the whole world. Painters don't make much money, Michael's father said. It was wiser to be a builder, or a banker. Or a butcher, or a grocer.

"Oh," Michael thought, "if only I could be the best painter in the whole world!"

Just then he heard a voice crying and grieving.

"I want my mother!" it cried and groaned. "Oh, oh, oh, I want my mother!"

Michael glanced around him in surprise. He had thought he was the only person on the beach. He could see nobody. But the voice sounded like a crying child.

Over the whole huge flat beach not a living soul was to be seen. And this was not surprising, for it was a cold frosty day in late September.

So where had the voice come from? It had sounded quite close at hand.

Michael searched and hunted, up and down, here and there. At last he realized that the voice seemed to come out of a turtle shell, which lay not far from his foot. Out of the shell poked a head.

"Was that *you* crying?" said Michael.

"Yes, it was. It was! They've taken my mother! They've taken her off to the zoo. Please won't you go and fetch her back?"

"I can't do that," said Michael. "The people at the zoo wouldn't allow me."

"Then take me to her. Oh please do, please, please!"

Michael didn't much want to do that. He would have preferred to stay on the empty beach, looking at the sea, and thinking about his future. But the turtle begged and prayed and pleaded, and then it said, "I'll give you a wish! You can wish for anything you want, if only you'll take me to my mother."

At that, Michael said quickly, "All right, I'll take you to your mother, if you will make me the best painter in the whole world."

"It's a bargain," said the turtle, pulling its head

back inside the shell. "Only carry me to the zoo. Main road to town, first gate on the left when you pass the station."

So Michael picked up the turtle and began walking. He was full of joy to think that he was going to be the best painter in the world. But after a while, he began to notice how very heavy the turtle was growing. He felt as if he were lugging along a sack of coal. Or a box of pig iron. Or a bucket filled with lead shot. And with every step it seemed to grow heavier. Michael began to be rather annoyed about it. "A bargain's a bargain," he thought, "but if I'd known how heavy the beast was going to be, I'd at least have gone home first and fetched a wheelbarrow."

He would have been even more annoyed if he had known that the turtle was not a real turtle at all, but a water kelpie playing a joke on him. Kelpies love to play jokes on people. And some of their jokes are not at all kind.

At last, panting and limping and staggering and

red in the face, Michael reached the zoo entrance.

There he stopped and began to wonder what he would say to the keeper. "I have a turtle here that says you have a turtle there who is the mother of my turtle. So will you please put my turtle with your turtle?"

He set the heavy, heavy shell down on the bank at the side of the road and said to it, "Hey, you turtle? When did they bring in your mother? Which day? And what is her name so that I can ask for her properly?"

But he got no answer.

"Come on, tell me!" said Michael. "Speak up! Which day did your mother get taken into the zoo?"

Still no answer.

Michael looked inside the shell, and was dumbfounded to find that it was bare and empty. There was no turtle inside, or anything else.

Very angry and puzzled, he left the shell lying on the bank and stumped off home. And when he told his father that a turtle had promised he should be the best painter in the world, and had then vanished, his father said, "I never heard such a peck of rubbish!" and sent Michael to work next day in a grocer's shop.

After a while Michael guessed that a kelpie had been playing a trick on him.

Work in the grocer's shop wasn't too bad. But just the same, Michael still wanted to be a painter, and so, in all his free time, though there wasn't much of that, he painted pictures. He painted the blue bags of sugar, and the white bags of flour. He painted the brown lumps of dates, and the piles of oranges, the green ginger, the yellow lentils, and the brown sticks of macaroni. He painted the red sticky cherries, the yellow butter, and the creamy cheese.

He painted so much, and so diligently, that by and by he began to paint very well. A traveling teacher, seeing one of Michael's pictures propped at the back of the grocery shop, offered to give him lessons. Michael worked hard at the lessons, and harder still at his painting.

After a while, people began to buy his pictures. So then he could stop working in the shop, and do nothing but paint. Indeed, people thought his pictures were beautiful; they were eager to buy them as fast as he could paint them.

After a while it began to be said that Michael was the best painter in the whole world.

By now, Michael had stopped painting groceries. No more currants or jam or flour or salt or lumps of butter. No, the pictures he painted were of rooms. A room with two chairs in it, or a table set with cups for breakfast, or a peaceful bedroom with the bed turned down tidily and a candle burning; or a playroom with toys scattered on the floor, or a kitchen with board and rolling pin set out, ready to make pastry. And each of these rooms looked so comfortable, so joyful, so welcoming and pleasant, that when you saw the picture, you just wanted to step right into that room and live there for the rest of your life.

Well! All this was fine, and time rolled along, and presently Michael was to hold a big exhibition, in a famous art gallery. There were to be all the pictures he had painted in the last few years. A van came to collect them all and take them to the gallery. And you may be sure that Michael went to make certain they had been hung up straight, not crooked, and not too high, and all in the right order.

And the first thing he gasped out, when he stepped inside the big room, was, "Murder! Who in the world has been playing the fool with my paintings?"

For into each of his beautiful pictures of a room, something new had been added. And what was that something but a great ugly kelpie!

A kelpie—you may know—is a huge horrid water monster, with the body of a horse, and the head of a cow, and two sets of teeth as big as gravestones, and enormous web-toed feet with claws on them as well. And it is all wet and hairy and whiskery and muddy and slippery and weedy and horrible. Of course, a kelpie *can* take any form it pleases, or vanish away entirely, but that is its real shape.

What a thing to see lolling in Michael's nicely turned-down bed, or squatting among the toys in the playroom, or munching toast among the broken plates on the breakfast table, or squatting by the sitting-room fire with its head turned and its eyes glinting, as if it were just waiting for you to walk into the room so that it could gobble you up! What a thing to find in the middle of each of Michael's beautiful, tidy, cozy, peaceful, welcoming pictures!

Poor Michael was in despair, and can you wonder? He didn't know what to do. He didn't dare face the owner of the art gallery, or the people who would soon be coming to look at his paintings, or the men from the newspapers who would be writing about them.

He ran out of the building and jumped on a bus, which took him to a train, and on the train he went back to the place where he had lived as a boy.

His father and mother were dead by now, and the old house had fallen down, but the beach was still there, and the sea was still there, green and thunderous, for a stormy wind was blowing hard and the waves were rolling in, big as castles, and crashing on the beach.

Michael walked along the shore and he shouted at the sea. "You cheated me! You promised that I should be the best painter in the world. You had no right to put your nasty self into my pictures!"

He heard a booming laugh come from behind him, and he spun around in a hurry. But there was nothing to see, only a big empty conch shell lying on the beach. Michael looked at it warily, and called, "Is that you in there?"

"It is I," boomed the kelpie. "And I never cheated

you. Did you keep *your* promise? Did you take me to my mother?"

"How could I?" demanded Michael crossly. "She was never there—you know perfectly well they don't have kelpies in zoos."

"You didn't keep your promise," the kelpie went on. "When I met you first, you were planning to paint a picture of the beach, this beach, with the green sea, and the gray sand, the waves rolling in, the white stones, the black breakwaters, and the golden hills. You have never painted that picture. And that was the one I wanted to see."

Michael stood and scratched his head.

"Well—that's true," he said at last. "I forgot all about it."

"Go home and paint that picture," said the kelpie, "and bring it here to me. And if I like it, maybe I'll see my way to taking myself out of all those kitchens and pantries and drawing rooms that you've been so busy putting into all your pictures."

So Michael left the beach and found himself a room at a pub, and he bought a roll of canvas and brushes and tubes of paint, and he painted a big picture of the shore, with all the waves, and the rocks, and the seaweed and creamy foam, the wintry hills behind, and the blue stormy clouds overhead, and a ray of light striking the sea like a spear.

Meanwhile, back in the city, everybody was hunting and searching for Michael. Why? Because his pictures of rooms with the hideous kelpie squatting in them had been a huge success. "What a talent!" people said. "What an imagination! What a strange, wild vision!"

All his pictures had been sold, for a great deal of money, and the art gallery owner was anxious for Michael to paint as many more as he could. Michael was wanted, too, for interviews on TV and in the newspapers.

But Michael, staying quietly at the pub and painting his picture of the sea, knew nothing about all this.

When the picture was quite finished, he took it down to the beach.

"Let's see, then," boomed a voice from a big razor shell, and so Michael laid the picture against a rock, and there was a long, long silence.

"Yes," said the voice at last. "That's the picture I wanted. Or very near it. I'll take it. You can throw it into the sea."

"*What?*" cried Michael in anguish. "Throw in my beautiful picture?"

"Keep it then," said the voice. "And you'll have me, too, for the rest of your life."

"No, no, you can have it," said Michael hastily, and he took the picture and hurled it far, far out, into the waves. They seemed to jump up and catch it among their curling crests.

"Good-bye, then," said the voice. "You won't be hearing from me again."

And when Michael picked up the razor shell, he found that it was empty.

So he took a train, and caught a bus, and went back to the city, back to the gallery. What a fuss and commotion he found there, for all the people who had bought pictures of rooms with a kelpie in them suddenly woke up one day to find that the kelpie had vanished clean away, and all they had was an empty painted room with nobody in it.

"Paint some more pictures of rooms with kelpies in—do!" the gallery owner urged Michael. "Everybody wants a kelpie!"

But Michael couldn't do that.

For he had never seen the kelpie, only heard its voice, and so he wasn't able to paint its portrait.

From that day on, Michael painted only pictures of the beach, hoping that the kelpie would come back and sit in them. But he never heard from it again.

The Spider in the Bath

Once there was a princess called Emma. Her father the king was a fussy, selfish man, always finding fault with the weather. If there were several hot days together, he would grumble, "When in the world is it going to rain?" If the wind blew, he said, "I can't stand this tiresome wind," and if it rained, he said, "Why doesn't the sun ever shine?"

He was so busy complaining about the weather that he had no time to spare for his daughter, who led a rather glum life. Her mother the queen had died when Emma was only two, and she had nobody to play with. The king would not permit her to play with the palace pages or the prime minister's daughter. Parcheesi, or dominoes, or Chutes and Ladders with the under nursemaid were the only games allowed her.

So Emma was often lonely and bored, and as lonely and bored people often do, she had become rather selfish and nasty.

The king's great-grandmother had been a witch, and Emma had a little seed of witchcraft in her—not much, but as she grew lonelier and nastier, the seed of witchcraft grew bigger.

When she was six, she discovered an interesting thing about herself. She found that, if she kept her whole mind very still, and thought very hard indeed, she could move small objects from one place to another without touching them.

For instance, she could move a pea or a potato chip from one side of her plate to the other, just by watching it and thinking about it and willing it to move.

She found this out by accident one day when the palace doctor had come to see her because she had a cold. He took her temperature and shook an aspirin out of a bottle, and was just about to pop it into Emma's mouth when the aspirin rolled out of his hand, fell on the floor, and bounced out of sight under Emma's bed.

"Confound it!" said the doctor. "Where's that pill got to?"

He shook out another aspirin, and that did the same thing.

Emma's face was perfectly straight, but inside she was laughing her head off. After he had lost four aspirins, the doctor, very annoyed, gave the bottle to the under nursemaid, Hattie, and told her to see that the princess had one before she went to sleep. He had better things to do with his time.

Of course Emma never took an aspirin. She detested medicine. And she could always get her own way with Hattie, who was very shy in her new job, only seven or eight years older than the princess herself, and a little frightened of Emma. With good reason. For soon, Hattie discovered that when Emma's cold blue eyes were on her, pins were likely to drop out of her fingers, or prick her sharply; buttons that she was supposed to be sewing on shirts would roll away and lose themselves; plates would slip from her grasp; or the hairpins would drop, all together, out of her shining hair, and Miss Targe, the head nurse, coming in and seeing Hattie's hair fall over her face, would scold her for untidiness.

Hattie soon began to suspect that the Princess Emma was the cause of these troubles, but how could she be sure? And anyway, there was nothing in the world she could do about it.

When Hattie played Parcheesi with the princess, the dice would be sure to roll over and over, giving the princess nothing but fives and sixes, while Hattie had a steady run of ones and twos. Also, Emma's counters seemed to skip ahead around the board by themselves, even when Emma's hands were nowhere near the table. When they played games, Hattie always lost.

After a while, Emma found that she was able to move larger things—oranges and apples and shoes and plates and hairbrushes. It was hard work doing this—she had to squeeze her mind together like a clenched fist inside her head, while sitting completely still, watching the thing she was trying to move. She had to hold her breath, and almost stop her heart from beating. The first time she managed to roll an orange from one end of the breakfast table to the other, she felt so tired that she had to go and lie down on her bed for half an hour.

But soon she grew better at her strange game. One day she even managed to move an apple right through the wall, from the nursery into her bedroom next door. Moreover, the apple went clean through the plaster without even leaving a hole! How about that! Emma was so proud of what she had done that she wanted to dance around the room and shout—but there was nobody whom she could tell.

The king her father would have said, "Quiet, please, Emma. Princesses should be seen and not heard," and then gone on grumbling about the weather. Hattie would have been scared to death, and worried as well. The palace pages would snigger disbelievingly. And the head nurse, Miss Targe, would say, "That's quite enough of that, Your Highness. We don't want such goings-on in our nurseries. Now go and wash your hands."

So Emma went on practicing by herself, in secret.

She moved a tooth out of her father's head, just before he bit into a piece of toast. She moved Hattie's fur bonnet onto the fire, one snowy afternoon, so the poor girl had to take Emma for a walk without it, and caught a nasty cold. Emma moved a rosebush into the middle of the palace lawn, greatly annoying the head gardener, who wondered for the rest of his life how it had happened. She moved a shoe from the hoof of one of the horses pulling the royal carriage, and a rolling pin from the cook's hand into the oven.

Sometimes Emma's trick went wrong.

You know how, if somebody knocks your elbow when you are pouring milk into a cup, the milk splashes all over the table. If some sudden sight or sound startled Emma when she was concentrating on moving an object, the result was rather queer.

The first time it happened was at lunch, when the footman set a dish of strawberries in front of the king. Emma fixed her mind on the dish, intending to move it just out of her father's reach, but a speck of dust on her nose made her sneeze, and instead of sliding away, the plate of berries shook and quivered and splintered and split up— so that suddenly, instead of just one dish, there were a hundred identical blue bowls, each full of red strawberries, lined up before the king in ten rows of ten.

He was furious, of course.

"Is this supposed to be some sort of joke?" he roared, and dismissed the cook, the butler, and all the footmen.

Emma wasn't in the least bit sorry for the people who had been sacked, just interested in what had gone wrong with her magic.

The same thing happened on a day when she was trying to move a narrow gold ring off Hattie's little finger. The ring had been left to Hattie by her mother when she died, and this annoyed Emma, whose own mother had left her nothing but a crown, which she would not be allowed to wear until she grew up. But the ring, a child's ring, very tiny, was tight on Hattie's finger, and in struggling to shift it, Emma's mind must have lost its grip for a second. The result was a hundred little gold rings glittering and clinking in the bathroom basin, which Hattie was doing her best to polish.

"My goodness gracious, Your Highness!" Hattie exclaimed. "Wherever in the world did all these rings come from?"

"Never mind where they came from. You'd better have them," said Emma crossly. "They are yours, in a way."

"No, indeed they are not, Your Highness." And Hattie carried them to Miss Targe, who scolded her, and whisked up the rings in her apron, saying they must have been left behind by a burglar. She took them to the palace security officer, who sold them and kept the money.

Still, apart from a few accidents like these, Emma, by regular practice, became more and more skillful at moving objects. By the time she reached her teens, she was growing ambitious and wanted to move live creatures. Think of moving a tiger out of the royal zoo! Or her father off his throne, out into the middle of the palace lily pond!

Emma found that moving live things was much harder work. She had to practice on very small creatures first, fruit flies, and the ants that ran over the palace terrace. Even houseflies were too large and fidgety. Bees, wasps, and bumblebees were too big, and their buzzing gave Emma pins and needles in her mind.

She still hadn't gone beyond ants when, one night, as she was getting ready for bed, she found a spider in her marble bath.

Emma detested spiders. And this was a particularly big one, black and furry and bunchy and long-legged. He kept very still indeed, but when he did move, when Emma's shadow fell across the bath, it was with such a sudden scurrying scuttle that Emma would not have dared touch him for anything in the world. She tried to move him with her mind; but he was much too big for that.

"Hattie!" Emma called loudly. "Miss Targe! Hattie! Come here quickly!"

But Hattie was out, for it was her evening off, and Miss Targe was downstairs having her supper.

Emma had to go to bed without taking a bath.

Next morning the spider was still there. He seemed to have grown a bit bigger.

"Hattie, take that spider out of the bath," said the princess, when the under nursemaid came in to lay out Emma's clean clothes for the day.

Hattie trembled a little—she was afraid of spiders too—but she carefully and gently wrapped the spider in a cloth-of-silver face towel and shook him out of the window onto the wisteria vine that grew outside.

"Now give the bath a good scrub before I get into it," said Emma.

At breakfast that day, among the mail, there was a letter from the crown prince of Pliofinland, asking for the Princess Emma's hand in marriage. The king snorted irritably over it.

"Who does he think he is? A miserable little

twopenny-halfpenny kingdom like Pliofinland! The prince who marries my daughter must bring a hundred gentlemen-at-arms, each one carrying a two-pound bag of diamonds. They certainly can't manage that in Pliofinland."

And he dictated a letter of refusal to his secretary.

Emma was delighted to think that her father valued her so highly. She spent the day trying to move a wasp out of a jam jar, and finally managed to shift it into a pot of face cream.

A month or so later, the spider was there in the bath again, and he seemed to have grown—to Emma's horrified eyes he appeared about as big as a plum. She tried again to shift him with her mind, but she couldn't.

Hattie was downstairs doing a bit of ironing, and Miss Targe was having her supper, so again Emma went to bed without her bath.

In the morning she ordered Hattie to kill the spider.

"Oh, no, Your Highness, I couldn't!"

"Go on, don't be such a coward!" said Emma crossly.

"It's bad luck to kill spiders, Your Highness!"

In the end, Hattie, trembling like a leaf, wrapped the spider in a golden towel, and carefully put him out of the window among the wisteria leaves.

"Throw him down on the terrace!" ordered the princess. "Otherwise he'll only find his way in again."

But Hattie was too kindhearted to do that. And Emma was secretly angry because Hattie had been brave enough to do something she couldn't do herself.

A few months later, when Emma went to bed, the spider was back in the bath again, and now he was big as a furry tennis ball with legs.

"Get out, you horrible thing!" said Emma, and she turned on the cold tap. The spider scurried to and fro in the bath as the water rose. His frantic movements frightened Emma, who thought he might jump right out of the bath. She turned the water off, switched off the light, shut and locked the bathroom door, and, without washing or brushing her teeth, jumped into bed, knocking over a glass of water on the bedside table. She hid her head under the covers, furious with the spider for having frightened her so.

"In the morning I'm going to move him," she decided angrily.

For that same day, at her practice, she had managed to move a canary chick and a small dormouse provided by the palace gardener.

"If I can move a mouse, I can move a spider," thought Emma. "I'll show him who's master."

So, the next morning, when it was light and she felt braver, Emma put on her ermine dressing gown and went into the bathroom, filled with determination.

There sat the spider, and he had grown in the night. Now he was big and hairy as a coconut.

Emma heard Hattie come into her bedroom with an armful of clean clothes.

"Now!" she thought, "I must do it quickly!" and she focused her mind on the spider like a gardener turning on a jet of hose water.

But just at that moment Hattie cut her finger on a piece of broken glass that Emma had knocked over and left where it lay.

Hattie let out a sharp cry of pain, and Emma's mind was jolted off its track. The spider in the bath jerked—quivered—fell apart—and, all of a sudden, instead of just one, there were a hundred huge black furry spiders, filling the bath to the brim, jostling and rustling and staring hard at Emma with their beady black eyes.

Emma let out a screech that brought Hattie running, with a handkerchief bundled around her bleeding finger. Hattie herself was so horrified by the sight of what was in the bath that she could only gasp, "*Oh!* Your Highness!"

"That was *your* fault," said Emma savagely. "So now *you* can get rid of them! Go on—that's an order."

She was furious that she had failed to move the spider.

Hattie, white as a cotton ball, stepped toward the towel rail, but Emma shouted, "No! You are to take those spiders out of the bath with your hands. I don't want those spiders touching my towel. Go on! Take them in your hands and drop them out of the window."

"Oh, Your Highness! You wouldn't make me do that!"

"Wouldn't I just!" said Emma. "Do it, or you're fired, and I'll see that you get sent to jail for disobeying my orders."

So Hattie, her teeth chattering with terror, crept to the bath, and plunged her hands to the wrists into the heaving furry mass of spiders. Her finger was still dripping blood.

"Well, one good thing," thought Hattie. "They

do say a cobweb's the best plaster to put on a cut.'' So that cheered her up a little.

She picked up a handful of spiders, all tangled together, and then, with her eyes shut, ran across to the window and dropped them out. Down they slid, on thick silvery webs, and left her hands all coated in web too, like gray silk gloves.

"Hurry up!" said Emma. "Don't stop. Get rid of them all!"

To and fro, to and fro Hattie went, with armful after armful of spiders. By the time she had carried half a dozen loads of black furry creatures, she found she didn't mind them quite so much. And presently she began to feel quite friendly toward them. After all, they were soft as thistledown, and they didn't bite, or sting, or even struggle, but just quietly let her carry them. Hattie, for her part, took tremendous care not to bruise them or bend their legs or bump them against each other, and she let each one glide gently down its own web onto the terrace below.

There were exactly a hundred.

As she let out the last one—"Oh, my goodness gracious!" cried Hattie. "Oh my word, Your Highness, do come and look!"

But Emma had flounced into the bathroom and was crossly brushing her teeth and didn't hear Hattie's cry of wonder.

Down below on the terrace, instead of a hundred spiders, there were a hundred handsome young men, all bowing and smiling. One of them had a crown on his head and a knapsack on his back; the rest carried plastic bags of diamonds. They all gazed up admiringly at Hattie's pink cheeks, blue print dress, and shining golden hair. The one who wore the crown bowed particularly low, and gave Hattie a specially warm smile. Even pinker than usual, she smiled shyly back.

"Who in the world are you all?" she asked.

"I'm Prince Boris of Voltolydia," replied the crowned one. "I was on my way here last year to ask for the princess's hand in marriage when my horse had the ill luck to tread on a snake who was a witch in disguise, and she turned me into a spider. She told me I could only be changed back by somebody who was brave enough to pick me up with their bare hands and kind enough to give me a little of their blood."

Hattie looked down at her bare hands, from which the silvery webs were peeling, and noticed with surprise that her cut finger was completely healed, although it had been quite a bad cut.

"So," went on Prince Boris, "I am forever grateful to you, dear and beautiful girl, for rescuing me, and I should like to ask for your hand in marriage."

"Oh!" said Hattie, blushing even more. "But I'm not the princess, I am only her maid."

"That," said the prince, "makes no difference at all. You are the lady for me. Will you ride back with me and be Queen of Voltolydia?"

"Yes, thank you!" said Hattie, for she had fallen in love with him at first sight, as he had with her.

So she pushed up the sash a bit farther, stepped out of the window, and slid down the silvery rope of spiders' webs, which was easily thick enough to support her.

"Who are all these other young gentlemen?" she asked, looking around at the handsome young men with their bags of diamonds.

"I have no idea," answered Prince Boris. "For some reason they all came and joined me in the bath."

"We wish to be your followers," chorused the young men.

"Certainly you may, if that is your wish," said the prince. "But you might as well leave all these diamonds here. We have enough diamonds in the mines of Voltolydia to keep the whole world supplied. I brought a bag to offer the princess. But what a disagreeable girl she is. I'm certainly glad that I was saved from marrying *her*!"

Boris and Hattie and all the followers jumped gaily off the palace terrace and hurried away to buy a hundred and one horses to carry them back to Voltolydia—where they lived happily ever after.

All that Princess Emma saw, when she had brushed her teeth and shouted angrily, several times, for Hattie to come and clean the bath, was a wide-open window. When she looked out she noticed, down below, a great many bags of diamonds.

No other prince ever came to ask for Emma's hand. Perhaps word had got around how disagreeable she was. She spent the rest of her life moving objects with her mind—larger and larger ones, until at last she was able to move whole cathedrals and power stations and icebergs and moderate-sized mountains.

At first she found it quite an interesting hobby, but in the end she became bored with it, and used to sit for days and days at a time on her throne (for by then the king had died and she had become queen) doing nothing at all whatever.

Think of a Word

Once there was a boy called Dan who was in the habit of using short rude words.

Almost any short word ending in T was rude in the country where Dan lived: Dit, Fot, Het, Rit, Sut.

"You silly old Sut," he called after an old lady in the street one day, and she turned around on him, quick as a whiplash.

"You'll be sorry you said that to me," she said.

"Why, you old Jot?" said Dan.

"Because, from now on," said the old lady,

"every time you say one of those words you seem so keen on, a tiny patch of your skin will turn to glass, so that everybody will be able to see all the works inside you. There are eight words that would cure the habit you have," she said, "but *I* shan't teach them to you. You'll have to find them out for yourself."

And she turned on her skinny old heel and walked away.

Dan was left standing there with his mouth open.

He didn't call anything after the old lady— somehow she had left him rather quiet and thoughtful—but later in the day, he forgot all about her, and called the driver of the school bus a stupid Nat.

"Dan!" said his friend Rod, who was sitting beside him. "Your face has gone all funny! I can see your teeth through your cheek as if it was glass. *And* the buttermint you're sucking. You didn't tell *me* you had any buttermints."

Dan, quite upset, couldn't wait to get home and look in the mirror.

Sure enough, a patch of his right cheek had gone clear and see-through—there were his teeth and his tongue, plain to view.

It was like having a plastic porthole in his face.

And after two or three days, a good few more patches had gone transparent all over Dan—on his arms, his legs, his neck, and even more inconvenient places. You could see bones and muscles in him, and tubes and joints and things that aren't usually seen.

The family doctor was quite keen to send Dan up to a big teaching hospital, so that the medical students could look at him and find out useful facts. But Dan's mother wasn't having any of that.

She was very annoyed about it, and so was Dan's father.

"It's disgraceful," they said.

So, since Dan couldn't seem to stop coming

out with short rude words ending in T, they took him away from school and sent him off into the mountains to be a shepherd.

High up in the hills, alone all day with the sheep, he couldn't come to much harm, they reckoned, as there was no one to talk to, and so he wouldn't be using any language, and, by and by, might learn to think before he spoke.

So off went Dan, into the high meadows, where he had no company but the baaing sheep and a surly old dog called Buff, who never barked, and who made it plain to Dan that he could have looked after the whole flock perfectly well on his own, without any help.

There, sitting on a rock, or on the short, sweet mountain grass, Dan had plenty of time to think, and to wonder which were the eight words the old lady had meant.

Day after day he thought, week after week, and he never spoke.

Thoughts piled up inside his head like leaves in

a hollow tree. He thought about how you could tow away the wind, if you had a strong enough rope. He thought about how, if you laid your plans carefully, you could win summer or winter to be your very own. He thought about rolled and stuffed thunder, and pan-fried lightning. He thought about weaving a rope of rain. He thought about the air, which is everywhere. He thought about the earth, which is nothing but a shepherd's pie of everything left over.

"Words are stronger than blows," he thought. "And perhaps," he decided later on, "thoughts are stronger than words."

So Dan passed days and weeks and months, wandering among the hills with his sheep. He was happy now. He didn't even want to go back to his home.

He listened to what the wind had to say, he watched the dark and the light playing hide-and-seek with each other, he felt the rock under his toes, he tasted the rain and smelled the warm salty wool of the sheep.

Meanwhile, down in the plains, and in Dan's home town, they were having a lot of trouble with dragons.

Dragons had suddenly started breeding quicker than wasps, and the whole country was full of them. Put your Sunday roast in the oven, and half an hour later a dozen dragons would have smelled it out; they'd be battering at your window like bulldozers.

Dragons fouled up the airport runways with clawmarks and scattered scales and droppings; they burst into banks and snatched bags of cash; they came snorting into cinemas and burned up reels of film; they broke off TV aerials and scraped tiles from roofs; splashing in rivers, they turned all the water to steam; they swallowed down hundreds of men, women, and children going about their daily affairs. And as for princesses—there wasn't a single princess left free in the world, for the dragons had collected the lot, and had them all shut up together in a nasty greasy cindery castle, which stood on an island in the middle of a lake, up among the highest peaks of the mountains, which in that part were so tall and sharp that they looked like the spikes of a king's crown.

Dan knew nothing of all this.

He did notice, to be sure, that dragons flew overhead much more than they used to: All of a sudden there would be a big spiny shadow across the sun, and the sheep would bleat in fright and huddle together, and old Buff the sheepdog would growl and snake out his head with flattened ears.

Dan noticed, too, that knights and princes and soldiers were quite often to be seen, riding horses or tanks or motorbikes up the highways into the mountains. From his perch on a high crag Dan would see them go up, but he never saw them come down again. Up, up, the tiny figures went, and vanished into the high passes. Maybe they

were crossing the mountains to the other side, Dan reckoned. He didn't give them too much thought. Nor did he trouble his head about the distant rumblings and flashes from those high peaks where they went. A bit of bad weather in the mountains was nothing out of the ordinary. The sheep didn't mind it, nor did Dan.

But one day a young fellow in shining armor, a handsome lad with a ruby-hilted sword and a gold crown around his helmet, came riding past the crag where Dan sat with his flock.

"Good day, shepherd!" called the knight. "Am I going right for the dragons' castle?"

Dan had to work his jaws and his throat and his tongue for quite a few minutes before he was able to answer—so many months had it been since he had spoken last.

"Umph—dragons' castle?" he croaked out at last. "Dragons' castle? I'm not sure I know of any dragons' castle."

"Oh, come *on*! You must know of it! Where

they have a hundred princesses shut up together inside—and a hundred dragons on the rampage outside. You mean to say you live up here in the mountains and you haven't heard of that?"

"I mind my own business," croaked Dan.

But when the knight told him that the castle clung like a cork in a bottle to the tip of a steep island in a mountain lake, Dan was able to set the knight on his right way.

"Up the pass, keep left, around a mountain shaped like a muffin—that'll take you there."

"*You* seem to live here safe enough, shepherd," said the knight, rather surprised. "Aren't you afraid for your flock, with so many dragons about?"

"They can't land here. The slopes are too steep," Dan told him. "A dragon needs a flat landing strip, or a stretch of water. Or a big rock that he can grab hold of. Slopes are too slippery for them."

All this Dan brought out very slowly. Finding the words was hard work, and tiring, like a walk through deep mud.

"I can see that you know a lot about dragons," the knight said, looking at Dan with respect. "I wonder—can you suggest any way to deal with them?"

"Dragons don't trouble me," mumbled Dan.

"No—but when I meet one of them—what should I do?"

Dan began to wish that the stranger would go away and leave him in peace.

"Oh," he said quickly—anything to get rid of the fidgety young fellow—"just write a word on your forehead with the tip of your finger dipped in morning dew. If you do that, then you'll have power over the dragons."

"Well, fancy, now!" said the knight. "What word should I use?"

So Dan quickly told him a word, and he set spurs to his horse and shook the reins. But then, pulling back, he turned and called, "Don't *you* want to come and rescue those hundred princesses?"

Dan shook his head, and the knight galloped away up the pass.

Sitting down again, Dan gazed at his flock, peacefully nibbling and munching. What? Rescue a hundred princesses? Not likely! Just think of the chattering and giggling and gabbling—the very thought of it made his head buzz. But still, he wished good fortune to the young knight. And now he began to feel a trifle anxious and bothered; for the advice he had given was thought up quite hastily on the spur of the moment. The words had come into his head and he had spoken them. But he hadn't the least notion in the world whether the idea would work or not.

"Maybe I ought to go after that young fellow and tell him not to try in case it doesn't work," he thought. "Only, if I did that, who would keep an eye on my sheep?"

Buff opened one eye and gave a bit of a growl.

"What's troubling Buff?" Dan wondered. "Are there more strangers about?"

And then he turned around and noticed a skinny old lady perched nearby on a ledge of rock. Quite comfortable she looked, and as if she had been there a good long time.

"Found out the use of words, have you, then, Dan?" said she cordially. And Dan answered her right away, as if the answer had been tucked away in a cupboard of his mind, waiting for this moment: "Trees are swayed by winds, men by words."

"Right," said the old lady, nodding her head energetically. "And now you've learned that, don't you forget it, Danny my boy. But," she went on inquisitively, "what was the word you told that young fellow to write on his forehead?"

"That was a word for *him*," said Dan. "Not for any other."

"Right again," said the old lady, nodding some more. "Words are like spices. Too many is worse than too few. Learned a bit of sense, you have. Remember it, and maybe you'll be some use in the world by and by." With that she vanished, like a drop of water off a hot plate, and Dan picked himself a blade of grass and stood chewing it thoughtfully, looking at where she had been.

Next morning early, Dan heard a distant sound that was like the chirping and twittering and chattering of a thousand starlings. And gazing down at the main highway that led out of the mountains, he saw them going past—what seemed an endless procession of princesses, with their fluttering ribbons and laces and kerchiefs, cloaks and trains and petticoats and veils a-blowing in the wind. A whole hundred of them, in twos and threes, jabbering and jostling, singing and laughing and giggling, down the rocky pass.

"I'm glad I'm up here, not down there," thought Dan.

But by and by, he heard the tramping of a horse's hoofs, and here came the young knight in his gold crown, with a princess, very young and pretty, sitting pillion on the saddle behind him.

And a droopy dragon following them, at the end of a long cord.

"It worked!" shouted the young knight joyfully. "It really worked! A thousand, thousand thanks! I'm everlastingly grateful to you—and so are all the princesses."

The one riding behind him smiled down at Dan, very friendly. She didn't seem to notice the glass patches all over his skin.

"Won't you come down with us to the city?" said the young man. "I shall be king one day, and I'll make you my prime minister."

"No, I thank you, Your Worship," said Dan. "I'd sooner stay here. Besides, people might not respect a prime minister with glass patches all over him. But I'm much obliged for the offer. Only tell me," he went on, full of curiosity, "what happened?"

"Why! As soon as the dragons saw the word written in dew on my forehead, they all curled up and withered away in flakes of ash! All except this one, which I'm taking to the zoo. I'd say," the knight told Dan, "there wasn't a dragon left now between here and the Western Ocean. Which is all due to you. So I thank you again."

And with that he set spurs to his horse, and started slipping and sliding, with the dragon limping along behind, and the princess waving thanks and blowing kisses to Dan, until they were out of sight.

All the time they were in view, Dan stood gaping after them. Then he slapped his thighs. Then he began to laugh, and he laughed so hard that he fell down, and Buff stared at him in disapproval.

"It worked!" shouted Dan. "It really worked! Dragons are bound by cords, and men by words."

He lay laughing up at the sky, with the larks twittering overhead.

Then he thought, "What word shall I think of next?"

He damped his finger in the morning dew and wrote on his own forehead.

A growl of thunder rumbled above him, and a lance of lightning flashed like a knitting needle out of a black ball of cloud.

"All right, all right," shouted Dan, waving gaily to the sky. "Just keep calm up there, will you? We won't have any of that for the moment. One word at a time is enough."

And he sat himself down on a rock to watch his sheep.

About the Author

JOAN AIKEN is the author of over three dozen books for young readers. THE WOLVES OF WILLOUGHBY CHASE won the Lewis Carroll Shelf Award in 1965. In 1969, THE WHISPERING MOUNTAIN was named runner-up for the Carnegie Medal, and it won the *Guardian* Award for Children's Fiction. NIGHT FALL won the 1972 Edgar Allan Poe Award, given by the Mystery Writers of America. Her most recent novel, MORTIMER SAYS NOTHING, is the latest in a series of books about a raven.

Ms. Aiken divides her time between homes in Sussex, England, and New York City.

About the Illustrator

ALIX BERENZY was born in Queens, New York, and attended Ohio's Columbia College of Art and Design and the Philadelphia College of Art. In addition to a number of beautiful jacket illustrations for a variety of books, more examples of her unusual black paper technique can be found in AMERICA'S VERY OWN GHOSTS by Daniel Cohen (Dodd).

Ms. Berenzy currently lives in Philadelphia, Pennsylvania.